# Liam Shark Boy

## by
## Stephanie Marie
## Roberts

*'Why fit in when you were born to stand out?'*

~DR SEUSS (1904 – 1991)
WRITER

REVIEWS: If you enjoyed this book, please write me a review on Amazon Kindle or my Website. Thank you!

Website:  https://www.stephaniemarieroberts.com
Facebook: https://www.facebook.com/StephanieRobertsAuthor/
          https://www.facebook.com/StephanieRobertsWriter/

ISBN: 978-0-6485363-8-3

Dedicated to


Liam

My magical Shark Boy,
who shares my love of all creatures of the world. I am happy you are part of my life and I am of yours.

~Nanny ღ

# Liam's Family

"Hup, Hup boys, c'mon get dressed if you want to come with me on the boat," called Liam's dad.

Four-and-a-half-year-old Liam hopped out of bed, his blue eyes as big as saucers, shining with excitement. "Can I feed the sharks?" he asked.

"Sharks are a bit dangerous my son. But if we are lucky, we may find one today," his dad, Steve said gently. He knew his little boy loved the ocean and the deep sea creatures. Liam wanted to talk to all of them, but he particularly liked sharks. He wished he could be a shark himself and swim with his beloved ocean creatures. Julie, his mum, was a bit nervous of her young son's enthusiasm for sharks but didn't want to frighten him about something he seemed to love so much.

"I'm not going," mumbled six-year-old Josh sleepily and turned over in bed. He did not share his brother's enthusiasm for sharks and the ocean. Harvey, the eight-year-old Cocker Spaniel, loved the excitement of the morning rush and danced doughnuts!

Liam pulled on his jeans and T-shirt back to front and yelled, "I'm ready!" "Brush your teeth Liam!" mum said sternly, pulling his T-shirt off and putting it back on the proper way, while he flailed his arms about.

"Ok mum," he grinned and dashed into the bathroom. He squeezed toothpaste on his brush, not worrying about it going all over the basin. Mum would be cross, but he would be gone! She'd be busy looking after his 3-month-old baby brother, Nicholas and forget about it by the time he came home. She would be proud of him when he told her he had talked to a shark and fed him some fish, Liam thought.

"Bye mum, see ya Josh!" Liam yelled as he dashed out the front door.

"Be careful my son," said Julie grabbing his arm and planting a kiss on his forehead. Josh was snoring, back in a dream world again.

# The Shark

The day was sunny and the water calm and glistening like diamonds, as Steve pulled in the anchor and untied the boat from the jetty. Liam helped his dad pull in the rope. "Well done," Steve said, patting Liam's head. "Put your cap on son, it's going to get quite hot soon."

The 27 foot Kingfisher Offshore boat moved smoothly on the high sea.

Liam sat strapped to his seat with his safety harness and floats, looking out into the water hoping that a shark would appear. Dad Steve cast his fishing line and waited, whistling happily.

"Look dad, a turtle!" exclaimed Liam.

"That's a Sea Turtle son. They have lived in the ocean for millions of years," explained Steve. "See how they swim by scooping water behind them? They can swim for miles, but don't get tired as their hearts beat slowly."

Just then, a brightly coloured Sea Anemone drifted past. "Isn't the big spider pretty Dad?" Liam said pointing to the sea creature.

"That's a Sea Anemone, Liam," said Steve. "Animal?" asked Liam.

"A-nem-a-ni, it has spiny shells, but no bones," explained Steve slowly. "Small feelers come out the top. They are called tentacles."

"I like the pretty A-nem-a-ni with his spectacles dad," Liam said, nodding his head.

"They can move, but very slowly," smiled Steve. "A balloon fish dad!" shouted Liam.

"That's a Jellyfish son," his dad said. "He has no bones. Just opens and closes his balloon to travel. He has little arms."

Steve's line tugged as a fish took the hook. Turning away from his son, he excitedly started playing the fish and reeling it in.

Liam's eyes which were fixed on the water saw a great snout appear followed by a big, big face with sharp teeth! It was a shark. The biggest shark he had ever seen. Bigger than all the sharks in the aquarium that dad took him to see. Steve didn't notice as he was busy with the fish on his line. It was a big one and he was determined to reel it in. He could boast to all his friends about the big fish he'd caught!

The shark came up to the side of the boat. Liam was so close to him, he could almost touch him! It was the biggest shark in the ocean, the Great Whale Shark. "Hello," Liam whispered softly. He didn't want his dad to hear him. Their eyes met and something magical happened. Liam's big blue eyes started to shine and beamed into the shark's eyes.

The shark spoke to him. "My name is Dearborn. Don't be afraid of me, I won't hurt you. You are a special boy, a Shark Boy. We'll meet again soon." Then he disappeared beneath the sea.

Just then, Steve reeled in the fish, a good-sized Ocean Trout. Julie would be proud of him. It would make a nice dinner tonight.

"Did you see that son? He put up a good fight, but I brought him in!" Steve said proudly.

"Dad, I spoke to a great big shark, his name is Dearborn," Liam replied, more interested in *his* encounter.

"Really, how nice son. Let's head on home now," said Steve, looking at his son with a smile. Liam and his love of sharks led him to fantasise about them all the time, he thought.

The boat headed home. Liam had bonded with a Great Whale Shark called Dearborn!

Maybe Joshua would believe him.

# The Magic Begins

That night Liam couldn't sleep. He was very excited! He lay in bed staring at the galaxy of glow-in-the-dark stars on the ceiling of his bedroom.

He had talked to a shark!

Suddenly his eyes started to shine like beams and propelled him out of his bed. Out into the night, they took him, flying over the treetops and the houses with

children fast asleep in their beds. He was heading towards the beach.

Whoosh! He landed on an ocean wave and started to sink down, down, to the depths of the sea. But he wasn't afraid, and he found he could breathe. He felt just like a fish.

"Hello Liam," said a deep voice. Turning his high-beam eyes towards the voice, he was surprised to see his friend Dearborn, the Great Whale Shark.

"I knew you would come, because you're a Shark Boy," Dearborn said. "Come with me. We have work to do."

Liam swam beside Dearborn, who took him deeper down to the ocean bed. It got darker down beneath the sea, but Liam's eyes beamed brightly and led the way. They arrived at a beautiful coral reef. There were red and yellow, orange and blue coral and all sorts of plants of the sea, which looked alive. A circle of little blue lights moved, and a small voice greeted Liam.

"I'm Goutoumi and I'm a Blue Spotted Stingray," it said. Liam was startled to see two eyes and a flat saucer-shaped body full of twinkling lights floating in front of him. "Hello Goutoumi, pleased to meet you," he said. Right behind him a red and white Lion Fish emerged. He was very regal as he sailed out with his red and white stripes. "Maximillian Forbes is my name," he said in his imperial voice. "Dearborn told us to expect you Shark Boy."

"Oh," said Liam excitedly, "I'm glad to be here." "Have you seen Pufferbee today?" asked Gotoumi.

"He's probably gone to see his grandad. He's not doing too well. His prickles are wilting and falling off. He's nearly ten years old, which is very old for a Puffer Fish," Maximillian Forbes informed them.

"I'm nearly five years old," said Liam. "People are only kids when they are five."

"How strange!" Goutoumi exclaimed.

A little Porcupine Puffer Fish swam up to them.

"Here he comes. Hello Pufferbee, we were just wondering where you were," Goutoumi and Maximillian Forbes yelled out.

"I went to visit Grandpuff. I took him some nice worms to eat, but he wasn't too hungry. Docpuff came to see him and gave him some seagrass medicine that

made him feel better. He fell asleep and was snoring when I left," Goutoumi said.

They arrived at a pretty cave filled with all kinds of algae and seaweed and small, colourful fish. "This is my home," Dearborn said proudly. Goutoumi and Maximillian Forbes rushed off to play catch with the fish. They were just playing and were not going to eat them Pufferbee said.

A Great White Shark was hovering over two baby sharks in the cave. "This is Ayala, my beautiful lady. She has just had twin boys," said Dearborn lovingly.

Liam went over to cuddle them, and they snuggled against his belly. They felt like his baby brother Nicholas, when he lay on top of him.

"Gather around Goutoumi, Ayala, Pufferbee and Maximillian Forbes," said Dearborn. "Liam Shark Boy has arrived. We knew he would come to help us soon."

"What do you need my help for?" asked Liam.

"The Bandit Sharks, Bolt and Storm of Qlort Deep, are terrorising humans swimming in the ocean," Dearborn informed him. "We must save them from having their legs bitten off and eaten up. Will you help us Liam?"

"Of course I will be happy to help," Liam replied. "But I'm not sure what I can do. I'm just a little boy."

"You're a Shark Boy with magical powers. You will soon find out," Ayala

promised him nuzzling his head. "Now you better go back to your bed before everyone wakes up in the morning."

# Grampy

Next morning at breakfast Liam wondered if anyone would believe him if he told them about where he had been last night.

"Maa...m," Liam started to say slowly, "guess what!"

"What Liam? Hurry up and eat your porridge or you will be late for school," his mum said crossly.

"Mum, I went deep into the sea last night and talked to Dearborn, my friend the Great Whale Shark," Liam announced excitedly.

"You didn't!" retorted Joshua. "It was just a dream."

"How nice son, now go and brush your teeth," Julie said with a smile. It wouldn't harm to let her young son pretend he talked to sharks, she thought.

"Can I visit Grampy tomorrow, Mum?" Liam asked. "Its school holidays and I could stay over for a few days." Julie was worried about her father now that his wife had passed away and she knew he loved having his grandson to visit. "Yes, I suppose you can son. Josh is off to his first school camp tomorrow so you will be lonely."

Yay!" said Liam, jumping up and spilling his milk. "Sorry mum, I'll clean it up."

Liam's grandfather lived by himself about 30 kilometres away in a small country town. He was very lonely since Nanny died and went to heaven last year.

Liam loved to visit his grandfather and Grampy Andy loved to have his favourite grandson stay.

Liam and his mum, with baby Nicholas and Harvey, who loved riding in the car, arrived at Grampy Andy's at 10:00 o'clock the next morning. Grampy was pruning his roses. He grew the most stunning roses and entered them in the garden show each year. Last year he had won second prize. He hoped to have a red ribbon pinned on his prize Queen Elizabeth rose this year. The red ribbon is first prize.

"Grampy!" shouted Liam rushing out of the car and hurling himself at his granddad. He was a burly, jolly man with a big moustache that Liam loved to tickle. Grampy Andy gave Liam a bear hug and said, "I'm going to crush your bones!" as he always did. Liam tickled Grampy's moustache and planted a big kiss on his nose

Julie kissed her dad on the cheek. Grampy poked Nicholas in the tummy and he chuckled back at  him.

"I'll pick up Liam on Saturday after I fetch Joshua from camp dad," Julie called as she headed back to the car, blowing Liam a kiss.

That night after dinner, as his granddad tucked Liam into bed, he told Grampy Andy about the shark and Grampy believed him! Grampy *always* believed him, Liam thought. Not like everyone else who believed he was just making up stories.

"Will you come with me to meet Dearborn tonight Grampy when he calls me?" asked Liam.

"Yes Lumlums," Grampy whispered gently, calling his grandson by his special pet name. Liam liked his special name that only Grampy called him. "Now go to sleep until you hear from Dearborn."

# The Adventure Begins

It was two minutes to midnight when Liam shot upright awake with a strange feeling. The magic was working. His eyes started to shine and he saw Dearborn in their reflection.

"Hello Liam," Dearborn said. "Bolt and Storm, the bandit sharks are on the prowl in Qlort Bay waiting for the little boys who are camping near the beach.

They are going for a swim at 7:00 o'clock tomorrow morning. You must come and help us protect them Shark Boy."

"I don't know what I can do Dearborn, but I'll come. Can I bring my Grampy because he believes in you?" asked Liam.

"If your Grampy believes, he can come with you Liam and your magic will protect him," Dearborn said.

"Oh goody, Grampy will love to come with me. See you tomorrow Dearborn!" Liam answered excitedly.

Early the next morning, Liam hopped out of bed and rushed to his granddad's bed, but Grampy was not there. Where was he? He was already up and outside watering the garden and feeding the birds. He was an early riser.

"Grampy, we have to go down into the ocean. Dearborn needs me and he said I could bring you," Liam said.

"I don't have your magic Lumlums. You go and I'll be here when you return, with a hot bowl of soup for lunch to warm you up," Grampy said.

"My magic will protect you Grampy. Let's go, there's not much time!" Liam shouted.

Liam stood very still and focused his eyes on Grampy. They grew as big as saucers and started to beam, enveloping Grampy in a blue light.

Oops! Grampy dropped the hose and water went everywhere! He and Liam took off into the air, flying over the house heading towards the ocean. Birds fluttered out of their way in surprise. A jogger nearly fell over looking at the strange sight of Grampy and Liam flying overhead!

Landing on a crest of a wave down, down under the sea they went, together.

Grampy was astonished he could swim and breathe underwater.

"Look Lumlums, isn't it enchanting down here. All these colourful fish and coral," Grampy exclaimed.

"C'mon, we have work to do Grampy, you can see all that later," Liam yelled back at him underwater.

# The Sharks of Qlort Bay

Dearborn was waiting for them in the cave. Ayala and the baby sharks were asleep. Pufferbee, Maximillian Forbes and Goutoumi were all also anxiously waiting for Liam's arrival.

"Hello Dearborn, this is my Grampy Andy," Liam told him proudly. "I love him very much. He believes in magic."

Grampy looked at Dearborn the Great Whale Shark and his eyes opened wide with wonder.

"You're BIG Dearborn!" he exclaimed.

"He's very kind Grampy, don't be scared of him," Liam assured him. "We are happy to meet you Liam's Grampy!" shouted Pufferbee,

Maximillian Forbes and Goutoumi all together.

"Are you a walrus Grampy?" Pufferbee asked. "I like your moustache." "No, I'm just a granddad, Pufferbee," smiled Grampy.

"My Grandpuff is sick. He's very old," Pufferbee said sadly.

"I'm sorry to hear that Pufferbee," Grampy said, hugging the little stingray. "Maybe you can take me to visit him."

"Later," interrupted Dearborn. "Now rally around my team, we need to get to Qlort Bay. Hop on to my back Grampy and Liam." Dearborn lay down on the ocean floor to make it easy for Liam and Grampy to climb on his back. Up, up the Great Whale Shark swam to the top of the ocean.

He blew a great big spout of water as he came up to the surface and nearly knocked Liam and Grampy over! Pufferbee, Maximillian Forbes and Goutoumi clung on to his tail for the ride.

The school boys were swimming in a group between the flags. The teacher had told them not to leave the flagged area, but one little boy was disobedient.

He was a good swimmer and swam into the deep part showing off with his strong overarm stroke.

"Shark!" yelled Pufferbee. Liam dived off Dearborn's back under the sea.

A 5-foot Blacktip Shark was heading towards the boy's legs. It gets its name from the black tips and fringes to its fins and tail. Liam, with Pufferbee and Goutoumi riding on his head raced towards the shark. Pufferbee, the Pufferfish has a strong poison. One drop can kill. Goutoumi, the Stingray, has two venomous spines on his tail that shoot out his poison.

Liam blinked his eyes three times and focused them on the Blacktip Shark.

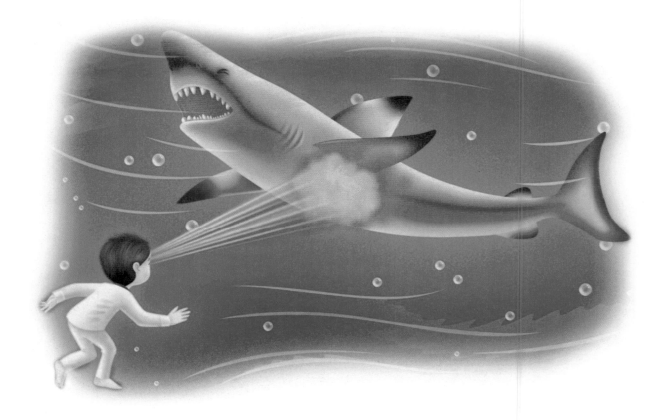

The beams started to burn a hole into the shark's stomach.

The Blacktip shot out of the water in pain with a great big yelp. As he landed back with a huge splash, Pufferbee spat some poison on his nose and Goutoumi swiped him with his tail stinging him. Blacktip took off leaving the little boy alone, who was shivering with fright and spluttering water. The lifeguard, who saw it all happen, reached the boy, grabbed him under the arms and headed back to the shore with him in tow.

Liam, Pufferbee and Goutoumi watched happily, giving each other a highfive!

"Well done," said Dearborn and Maximillian Forbes with Grampy, swimming up to them.

Liam and Grampy turned around to look at the boy to see if he had arrived safely. His eyes were closed and he didn't see them. But Liam and Grampy recognised him.

It was JOSHUA!

"Let's all go and visit Grandpuff," Grampy said, "to see how he's doing, before we go home."

Grandpuff was feeling much better and had eaten a worm or two. Grampy and Grandpuff hit it off straight away and became good friends.

See you next time." Grandpuff called, as Dearborn and the team, with their new leader Shark Boy, waved goodbye.

# The Next Day

"Did you bring back a boy?" Bolt asked Blacktip when he returned to Qlort Bay wounded and burnt.

No, Shark Boy has arrived Master," he said sheepishly. "His Magic defeated me.

Rubbish, there is no magic – fagic!" Bolt replied. "No one is stronger than us. You will bring Shark Boy to me next time. It is an order."

"Yes Master," Blacktip replied in a very small voice, slinking away to nurse his wounds.

When his Mum came to pick up Liam with Joshua, Baby Nicholas and Harvey next day, Liam hugged his brother Joshua very, VERY tight and Joshua hugged him back. They went to the car together laughing and punching each other as brothers do. Harvey danced doughnuts around them again as he did when he was very happy.

Liam turned around to wave to Grampy, who gave him a big WINK.

**_The End_**

# About the Author

Stephanie Marie Roberts writes children's books and romance. She is a Book Excellence Literary Award Winner and Silver Medallist for *Joshua's World* and *Liam Shark Boy.* She started writing for her little grandsons Joshua and Liam, which grew into writing for all the kids of the world!

Stephanie is also an incurable romantic. She was born in India in post Second World War days when children were seen but not heard, to parents of Anglo-Indian origin. Her father served as a dive bomber and fighter pilot in the India and Burma theatres of war during the Second World War. She has just released a heart-warming historic romance novel *Always* based on true incidents from her life.

Two beautifully illustrated books: a coffee table book of inspirations *When Love Finds You* and her heart book *The Well of True Gestures* helps couples bond in their relationship.

Stephanie lives on the beautiful Central Coast of Australia with her retired secret-service husband Chris and sixteen-year-old pampered Cocker Spaniel Harvey. Dogs are her passion and she must have a dog under her feet when she writes.

For hardcover coffee table version or any other paperbacks not available on Amazon, write to stephanieroberts@iinet.net.au to order direct.

These children have no classroom, just an enormous undercover area with a concrete floor. In winter, the wind blows through and in summer it is very hot. They have few picture books. They write on slates, always shared (no paper), but they are happy and eager to attend 'school'. They remain quiet when asked to, they wait their turn, patiently. They look after each other and comfort a child who may be crying or upset or stop to pick up someone who may have fallen over. They share what they are given to eat. These children have so little, yet they are so happy and contented.

20% of all sales go to Third World Children, for food, clothes and school supplies.
https://www.stephaniemarieroberts.com

Made in the USA
Coppell, TX
21 September 2023

21787416R10029